LOVE NEEDS A SECOND CHANCE

LOVE NEEDS A SECOND CHANCE, MAYBE IT WASN'T READY THE FIRST TIME AROUND.

NUZLA IMRAN

Contents

ONE
IT'S HIS DAY

It was on 15[th]of June 2020, Joseph woke up distressed with so much of depressions. He widely opened the wooden windows with crystal clear glasses that was deeply embedded in the dark blue, granite walled bedroom. The morning look was mind-blogging and it completely transformed his mind. Joseph was able to comprehended the reason behind it.

The fog filled in the entire garden outside to the slightest. The sparkling morning dew lit up the grasses like a colony of fireflies. It seemed as if the red roses were symbolically trying to tell him a 'good morning' with a radiant, flourishing smile. The sluggish breeze shook the trees and Joseph felt that the sound of breeze was a like melody to which the trees gave a dancing movement.

Joseph hoped that this entire day should be filled with surprises and love because it was his day. Yes, his 25[th]birthday.

"When nature is ready to grant me happiness, what's wrong with my blood and dudes?" Joseph mumbled and rummaged up and down for his mobile. He found it on the coffee table that was placed just below the 40" inch LED television that hung on the granite wall. He went through the messages but he didn't even find a single message that wished him on his great day.

Joseph shook his head with disappointingly. "I hope nothing is wrong with them," he muttered. He walked out of the room in his white pyjamas and blue T-shirt, with which he went to sleep last night.

Suddenly, he closed his eyes and held on his breath for a moment. The worst feeling that one could ever undergo is getting poured by water on a sleepy face. Who could do such irritating tasks? Joseph opened his eyes and raised his hand to punch the person who stood right opposite to him.

"Happy Birthday, dirty face!" squealed Amira, Joseph's one and only sister. She was so dear to Joseph as she was the one and only sibling he owed. Amira was short, cute and pretty. She possessed long hair though, it looked short as they were formed in curls. She possessed a childish behaviour. Though, she had frequent arguments and little quarrels with Joseph, she always had endless love and affection for her dearest brother.

"Look next time I'm gonna hold you by your neck and hang you on this wall," Joseph grumbled.

"Oh really...Thank you so much, Joe. You think that I am very gorgeous looking to be hung on the wall like a photo frame. You are the only one who is admiring my beauty all the time," Amira hinted at Joseph with a giggle.

"It isn't sarcastic. Remind me about it an hour later, so that I can laugh out loud. I know you will worry a lot if I don't," Joseph replied ridiculously and left the place.

Amira folded her palms tight and bit her cute tiny lips. "Buff...shit...for whatever I say, he is always ready with a witty reply...I am his blood but why can't I tease him just like he pokes fun at me?" Amira murmured angrily.

Joseph's father, Richard was busy reading the Sunday Times newspaper at the dining table. Although he was an authoritarian parent, Joseph and Amira loved him so much because he always shared his experience and struggles with his children and educated them on overcoming such tough circumstances in life. Richard was a retired clerk at his age of sixty-one, medium height and weight, with a nearly bold head. As a retired government officer, his favourite hobby was reading newspapers, magazines and novels most of the time.

Joseph walked into the kitchen to make a coffee for him. He saw his father was focusing through his spectacle so seriously into the newspaper. Before Joseph opened his mouth to tell a 'Good Morning', Richard spoke up, "Good Morning, My dear son. A very happy birthday to you. Have a blessed day, Joe."

"Thank you, Dad," Joseph replied solemnly.

Though Amira and Richard gave their heartfelt wishes to Joseph on his day, he still felt that the day was empty. The reason for the emptiness was his mom, he realized. His past birthdays were celebrated with the presence of his mom but his 25[th]birthday was not fortunate enough. Joseph missed his mom Regina to the core of his heart. Not only him, Richard and Amira too had the same emotion. But they buffed not to express anything in front of Joseph as it was his birthday.

Regina's demise nearly killed Joseph's heart eight months ago. She had suffered from a heart ailment for which enormous treatment were conducted. But, there was no use in it because God had wanted to take her life very soon. There is a saying 'God never leaves Good-hearted people for a long time on earth.' That was true with Regina.

She had a pure helping heart which everyone admired about. She was incredibly generous and kind-hearted. Words in the world were not enough to describe the love that she showered upon her family. Her loss pushed the entire family into deprivation. Joseph couldn't recover from the bereavement although, he tried a lot. He knew that birth and death were a part of the life equation but, losing his beloved mother was a painful experience he had to endure. Every moment at home reminded him of his mother. So, Joseph preferred to stay out of the house most of the time.

Joseph completely forgot the reason why he came to the kitchen. He went back to his room, worrying about his beloved mom. He began to observe the nature again while tears rolled down his cheeks.

"Triing...Triing..." The door bell rang.

"Who is here this early morning?" Joseph questioned to himself and went up to the door to check who it was.

Once he opened the door, he found that his friends were standing outside in their office outfits. Joseph attempted to ask if something was wrong but they interrupted.

"Happy Birthday to you...Happy Birthday to you...Happy Birthday to dear Joseph. HAPPY BIRTHDAY TO YOU...," Max, Bob and John sang in a chorus.

They held a pure white cake box in their hand and stepped into the house before Joseph had welcomed them. It was a complete surprise for Joseph. He looked at his father and Amira.

"It isn't a surprise for us. They already informed us about their arrival. They said that their arrival can give you excess happiness," Amira said with a glimmering smile.

Joseph looked at his friends with full of pleasure filled in his eyes. "Thank you so much, Dudes...This means a lot to me," Joseph thanked them heartily.

"Okay…now it's time to cut off the cake," Max clapped his hands and cheered up.

Amira opened the pure white cardboard box in which she found a beautiful circular rich moist chocolate cake, frosted with chocolate creamy whipping. It had been decorated with Choco brownish roses made with butter icing. The edge of the cake held some ganache that added an extra look to the cake.

Everyone sang a Happy birthday song and Joseph started cutting the cake. He shared the cake with all of them and had a great time.

"You guys made my day," Joseph said sympathetically.

"Enough, There is no time for emotions here. It's already eight. Get ready soon and we have got to go. I hope you know that chimpanzee will chew us if we don't," Max said simply without a reaction on his face.

"Chimpanzee?" Amira sniggered.

"Yeah, I am talking about Alex, our boss. We usually call him Chimpanzee," Max replied.

"But Why? He is your Boss, isn't he?" rudeness appeared in Richard's face.

"I do not disagree with it. But he acts like that. Poking his head into our cabins irritates us often. Not only that, when something goes wrong he scolds us in such a way which exactly looks similar to that of a chimpanzee's actions," Max said hilariously, to which everyone around cackled with laughter.

Max, Bob and Joseph worked in the same Software Company for two years and they had been good friends since then. Joseph loved spending most of his free time with them as they were supportive and comforting for him.

Joseph dressed up in his navy blue slim fit shirt and dark black jeans which his father gifted him soon after they had finished cutting the birthday cake.

Joseph was a handsome guy with a manly look. He was tall and fair with thick black straight hair. He had bristly eyebrows and sea rover- blue eyes. The aquiline nose complemented his cheekbones. His beard was smooth, spade-shaped. He wasn't a male model but he looked like it in the outfit which he had worn.

Joseph received heartfelt blessings from his dad and stepped out of his house with his pals saying a 'Bye'.

TWO
HER LOVE

Joseph's office was located twenty kilometres away from his residence. It usually took about thirty minutes to travel in a car. But when roads get jammed with vehicles, it almost took about an hour to reach there.

On the way to the office, Joseph complimented, "Thank you so much for the surprise, Guys. When my mom was alive, my birthday had been full of joys. I thought that this would not happen today."

John replied, "Be cool. I know you have been suffering a lot from the time your mom had passed away. But keep in mind that, someone, who is special will replace it very soon."

Bob interrupted, " Yes, he is correct. When your loved ones go away from you, it doesn't mean that your life is going to be disastrous till you die. Someone will get into your life and give rise to colourful flowers. I assure you, it may happen today, tomorrow or sooner."

But Joseph remained silent on their words.

"Not sooner or later. That person had already entered into his life," Max babbled in between.

Joseph, Bob and John looked at Max weirdly.

Joseph questioned, "What?" doubtedly.

"Yes, I am talking about Annie. Have you ever noticed Annie's facial expressions when Joseph is around? The way she gazes at him, the way she blushes at him. OH MY GOD...I know she has a sky-high fondness for him. I think it is the same with Joseph too, isn't it, Joe?" Max verified.

"OHSSS...shut up!... I don't have any kind of impression on her. She is just a friend of mine, that's all. And I don't think Annie does have such opinions on me as you think. She has her own goals and me too," Joseph replied in rage and continued, "You know that Annie had lost her father in an accident two years ago and now, she is responsible for her entire family. How can you imagine a girl falling in love with a guy like me in such a difficult condition, Max?"

Max remained like a muted phone.

"Today is my birthday and if Annie is really in love with me, she must be the first person to have wished me but she didn't. So never judge a book before you had known completely about it," Joseph clarified further.

"Okay...Okay...relax Joseph! Max is unaware of it. What he knows is to keep rocking with a box of jokes all the time. Neglect it. I hope that you will offer us a treat in the evening, am I right?" John tried to change the topic to defend Max.

"Yeah of course, Why not? Let's have dinner at 'La Barista' today. I will pick you guys by 07:30 p.m. So, Get ready on time."

"That's great, dude," cheered three of them.

It was sharp 9.00 a.m. when the crew reached the office. They saw Annie at the entrance holding a small box covered with a blue wrapper that was knotted by a silky gold ribbon. It seemed as if she was waiting for someone so eagerly. John got out of the car, led others and walked forward. "Good morning, Annie! What's up?" John asked.

"Good morning John! Ehhh...mmm...Nothing, I came earlier today, I was just loitering here and there," Annie replied hesitatingly glancing at Joseph through her hazel eyes. She hardly shifted her eyes from Joseph which he did not study.

Annie joined the software company two years ago soon after her father's demise. She became so closer to John, Max and Bob after her recruitment. But she always maintained a gap between Joseph and herself from the very beginning. The rapport she had with him was completely different. Many thought that the distancing was just because of Joseph's introverted character. But Annie knew that it was something unique from her point of view.

Annie possessed ebony-black hair and it flowed over her shoulders. But she always tied it in a ponytail. She had a shapely figure with glossy skin. Her slender eyebrows and velvety eyelashes just above her almond-shaped eyes were the most attractive part of her face. She had a dainty nose and honey-sweet lips. Her lips were blossom soft. Her voice was soothing. She was always simple in her dressing and behaviour as well. Most of the office staff say, 'Simplicity means Annie'. Everyone loved Annie for her cheerful character. Even some of the male staff at the office proposed to her but she rejected every one of them. The only reason was, she loved Joseph from the core of her heart. She knew him from the time she had joined the office. She admired him a lot from the beginning. His helping nature, kind heart and his decency towards women attracted her to the utmost but she always kept quite patiently about her love. She was afraid that Joseph would reject her if he is not interested and ultimately, she would have to lose her precious friendship too. That was the only complication that she had in her mind.

"Hello, little daydreamer! You never told that you gave up software engineering and shifted your job to a security," Max hinted.

"Oh No...Max! Stop it," retorted Annie.

"Instead of daydreaming, you can join us for dinner tonight at 'La Barista'. Don't worry about the currency. You can order as you wish and Joseph is going to pay for it as it's his birthday", Max invited Annie.

Joseph stared at Max and whispered into his ears, "What the hell? I never told you that I am going to invite her?"

Annie interrupted, "No...Thank you so much! I have some miscellaneous work at home tonight. I know it's Joe's birthday today. I wanted to wish him at 12:00 midnight. Unfortunately, my mobile wasn't working all of a sudden. I was helpless. I was waiting here to wish him. Happy Birthday, Joe," Annie handed over the box with the blue wrapper to Joseph along with her heartfelt wishes.

Max stared at Joseph and raised his eyebrows. Joseph put his head down for a while. He remembered what he said on his way.

'If she is really in love with me, she should be the first to wish me.'

"But still it isn't called love when she wants to wish and gift me for my birthday. It can even be for friendship," Joseph decided.

"Thank you so much, Annie!" Joseph responded and received her gift.

Annie gave a flashing smile and said, "You are always welcome."

Bob cried out, "It is unfair. Annie never gifted us on our birthdays."

Annie pondered glancing either sides thinking what to say while Joseph glared at Bob.

"Okay guys, Let's get back to work before the chimpanzee arrives here," Max called out and went inside. The crew cracked up and entered inside following him.

•

THREE
LA BARISTA

It was 07:35 p.m. when Joseph picked up his friends at their relevant locations.

"You are so punctual, isn't it? Late by five minutes," Max said sarcastically.

"Hmm...Just five minutes, isn't it?" Joseph said carelessly.

"Five minutes consists of three hundred seconds. Time is so valuable, Joseph. Histories declared that many people had failed in their life just because of time. Let me explain to you with an example. A guy missing the bus for an interview just because of delaying a minute, a girl missing an entire question in an exam paper due to five minutes late attendance. Dude, things should be executed on time and when we fail to do so, we shall face a great loss in the future," Max was indirectly explaining something which Joseph could not understand.

"Now what are you trying to tell?" Joseph shouted.

"Nothing," Max mumbled and closed his eyes pretending to sleep.

They entered La Barista at sharp 08:00.p.m. La Barista was a famous restaurant for rich delicious food in the city. It was well-known in the city due to its mind-blowing lakeside view. The restaurant was intimate and elegant with a dimly lit space that had an entire wall which was a fish tank. It contained milky white carp and goldfishes that swam back and forth. The opposite side of the fish tank had a wide opening which led the fresh air to enter inside. Through the wide opening, one could see the entire view of the beautiful lake as well. The whole restaurant was furnished with rounded dining tables which were carved with different colours of wood. One was coffee brown, the next was dessert brown, following that was a smoky topaz dining table.

The guys took over the seats on a dessert brown table. The waiter who was dressed in a pure white shirt with a dark black overcoat came closer to their table and handed over the menu. Joseph went through the menu and ordered a cheesy veg lasagne. Following that, Bob and Max ordered a non-veg pizza with pepperoni, mushroom, black olives and mozzarella toppings while John requested a Zinger burgher. For dessert, they ordered fudge walnut brownies. The waiter noted down the order and went back while Max, Bob and John went out to have a close up look at the ethreal lake. They forced Joseph too but he wasn't interested anymore.

Joseph sat isolated. He felt that the fresh air from the lake is paying calls to him once in a while inside the restaurant. He felt that he could have gone out with his friends to enjoy the fresh air in abundance by the lake side but, something stopped him from doing so.

He glanced at the opposite smoky topaz table abruptly. A girl was seated alone there. It seemed that no one had accompanied her. She was tasting double chocolate brownies with white chocolate dripples. He tried to have a look at her because she was captivating him too much but only half of her face was visible to him. She had a thick black, mid back length hair that flowed in long layers. She was alluring as well as gorgeous too. She was wearing a red bodycon which accentuated her shapely body with curves. She turned her face to the direction where Joseph was seated. This time, Joseph was able to see her more vividly than before. Her eyes were fabulous in her own way dark and attractive. She had thick pink heart-shaped lips that curved in bends. Her sight was breathtaking for him. Was it love or lust? He couldn't guess. She was looking steadily and intently at something that was at the entrance. Joseph could not find what it was. He was only able to see a smoky grey wagon. "Is she gazing at that wagon?" Joseph questioned himself.

But within a second, she fetched her golden wallet, stood up and went straight towards the entrance. Joseph did not want to leave her being anonymous to him. He followed her back as quickly as he could but unfortunately, he saw her getting into the grey wagon which he saw at the entrance a while ago.

The treat was over at La Barista and Joseph never spoke a word about that anonymous girl to his friends. His intention was not to hide it from them. He wished to find more about her and let them know.

He had an inexplicable desire for her. May be some strong love or affection, he couldn't understand. He spent a sleepless night that day. Thoughts of her were floating in his heart. He felt that he had become just like an insomniac.

"Please do wait for me. Very soon, I will find you, My dear girl," Joseph whispered.

FOUR

THE MISSING MOBILE

The next morning, Joseph woke up with heart-filled joy. The first thing that came into his mind was that anonymous girl whom he saw at La Barista. Usually, in the earlier days, he used to wake up with the remembrance of his lovable mom but that day, a particular girl had replaced it. He felt that his heart beated rapidly than usual. That someone about whom John and Bob discussed had just entered into his life. He was in love with her eyes, her looks, her body and most of all he was madly in love with her. She amazed him in every way. Joseph held his heart so tight.

"I have no time to spare thinking about her. My duty today is to find, who is she? What is her name? From where is she? Her marital status?" Joseph paused a minute.

"Obviously no...She is not married, I hope she shouldn't be, if she is, what will I do? OH MY GOD! I can't even visualize it...I love her so much. My worst fear is to lose her," Joseph babbled to himself.

Suddenly, he jumped out of his bed and rushed to the washroom. Within ten minutes, he got ready and headed towards his car.

"Wait...wait...wait...," Amira yelled.

"What's wrong? Why are you screaming as if your life is in danger?"

"Can you drop me at college today? My scooter is so hard to pedal and I am already running out of time."

"Come on...Get into the car."

The road was congested as usual and a number of vehicles were zooming past and some were even crawling along when caught at the traffic light. Joseph drove smoothly even on the hectic road. The red signal gleamed radiantly and Joseph had to stop there for a moment.

"Amira, Can I ask you a question?" Joseph inquired reluctantly.

"Yes, of course."

Joseph scratched his head and went on, "Ehhh...mmm...What type of sister-in-law do you expect? No...I am expecting your opinion."

Amira goggled at Joseph and said, "I...I...had never thought of it and I cannot express it with my words. But I have an individual in my mind. That is my friend Nancy's sister. I want a sister-in-law similar to her. Do you know why? She has an amazing personality. Affable, easy-going, smart and pretty as well. There is much to illustrate about her but we are badly lacking time now."

The red light shifted to green and Joseph moved his car again. On his way, he wished, why shouldn't Nancy's sister be that anonymous girl? If it is, his family would accept her with pleasure. His and Amira's wish is more important to his father and he wouldn't reject. "She too must possess a great personality," Joseph's mind voice echoed.

Joseph dropped Amira at her college and drove at a higher speed towards his office. He was unpunctual by twenty minutes so, he had to scurry off to his cabin. All of them were engaged in their work energetically and Joseph wasn't noticed specifically.

Annie, Bob, Max, John and Joseph usually sat together during lunchtime break. They would talk, crack some jokes and have lunch together. But on that day, Joseph found Max and Bob were seated in the room empty faced.

"Where are John and Annie?" Joseph questioned Max and Bob.

Both of them remained speechless.

"What's wrong? Reply to me?"

"Why should we respond to you when you don't answer our phone calls?" Max asked annoyingly.

Joseph rolled up his eyes and touched his pocket that was fitted in his jeans and shirt. "Phone calls...Did you call me? My mobile is missing," Joseph answered in a perplexed tone.

"Oh...you don't know where you kept your mobile? We have been calling you since 07:00 a.m. It isn't in your pocket and it isn't in your house. Then, where is it?" Bob questioned irritatingly.

"Please stop...I don't know. I should have put it in a silent mode. I had forgotten to take it with me to the office. What happened actually? Why did you guys phone me?" Joseph asked in a tension-filled mind.

"Annie's mom had had an unexpected heart attack in the morning today. She had phoned you a number of times and the calls were unanswered. Then, she had phoned John and asked for help from him to get her mom admitted in the nearby hospital," Bob explained.

"Oh My God...I feel pity for her. I...I really...Where is John now?" Joseph stammered.

"He is with Annie at the hospital. You know Annie has no one to assist her in such a tough time like this. Her sisters aren't that matured enough too. We are the only people who should console her and feed her with bravery to handle the situation tactically," Bob said.

"Yeah, that's true. Let's go straight to the hospital once the office time is over," Joseph suggested.

Bob and Max nodded their heads.

Joseph got back to his cabin. He had forgotten about his lunch as well. He was confused to the core because he had missed his mobile somewhere. He was hundred per cent sure that he neither put it in a silent mood nor switched off it. He lied to his friends so that they wouldn't doubt him. He never saw his mobile since last night from the time he came home from La Barista. He borrowed his cabin mate's mobile and dialled up his number a couple of times but there was no answer at all. He knew, he had left it on the dessert coloured table. He reminisced his actions yesterday sincerely.

When the angelic lady stood up and walked out, he left his mobile on the table and went after her up to the entrance. When he returned, he sat on another coffee brown table, ignoring the dessert coloured one. His friends too did not ask the reason and Joseph missed his mobile there.

"La Barista usually opens at 06:00 p.m. If I can get there at least by 06:20 p.m. I can get it back. But, what if one of the waiters there had already seized it? Exactly no. If it is, he should have switched it off but the mobile rings. It must be on the table. And there was no time left for the waiters to steal it because it was almost 11:54 p.m. when we departed the restaurant and the waiters had cleaned all the tables by that time. They were getting ready to leave home at the same time when we came out. If they had stolen it, I can catch them by the CCTV footage," Joseph explored.

It was 06:00.p.m. and many of them started to leave their cabins. Max and Bob got into their car and waited for Joseph to come. It was almost 06:15 p.m. but Joseph did not come. They became tired of waiting for him at a point. Max went back into the office again in search of Joseph. Joseph's cabin-mate informed him that Joseph had already left at 5:50 p.m.

Bob saw Max walking back to the car in frustration. He reacted in such a way asking what happened, symbolically by frowning his face and turning his palms anteriorly.

"He had left from here twenty five minutes ago," Max replied tartly.

"What? He didn't inform us. He doesn't even know the name of the hospital," Bob gaped.

"Mmmhh...He has gone somewhere. It isn't his mom, am I right? That is why he is careless about it. Anyway, Let's go to the hospital. Annie and John must be waiting for us to come," Max hurried. Bob nodded and they headed to the hospital.

Joseph reached 'La Barista' at 6:10 p.m. He scuttled towards the dessert brown table and rummaged for his mobile but, all in vain. It wasn't available there. He held his hair tight with both of his palms and bit his teeth in rage. He turned to the other side and looked everywhere. The restaurant seemed empty and there were no customers. He immediately went to the manager, explained the matter and requested permission to have a view of the CCTV footage but the manager refused to show unless he comes with the police.

"There is no use of arguing with them here. They are some kind of offenders. One of the waiters here must have ripped off it," Joseph decided.

Joseph walked out of La Barista and took a deep breath. He glimsped at the opposite side of the busy street. There stood a small bus stand with long wooden benches where the passengers were seated. Something fascinating caught his eyes. That was she, the anonymous angel. She was sitting on the wooden bench waiting for someone. She looked different from what she was yesterday. She was wearing a golden yellow, flow length, silky frock designed with red roses made with ribbons. Unlike yesterday, she had hung a medium-sized, leather handbag on her shoulders. Her hair was flirting with the cool sunset breeze.

Joseph felt that his heart was cold and hard like an ice cube kept inside a freezer. His eyes widened more and more, just like the mouth of a river flowing into the ocean. And finally, his heartbeat rose. His heart strongly ordered 'Run...Run... Towards her right now.' Joseph stepped his feet one step front to walk further but within a moment, a red Mercedes-Benz stopped right in front of the bus stand. The anonymous angel stood up, came closer to the car, opened the door and got into it. The car took off.

"Who is she? A billionaire, a model or an actress? Yesterday in a grey wagon and today in a Mercedes-Benz. If she is a distinguished businesswoman in the city or a model, I should have known her. Yet, her face is completely new."

Joseph had tons of questions to be answered by her and his curiosity increased to the top.

FIVE

COSTA COFFEE SHOP

Joseph went home after a tiresome day. Everything seemed like a dream. He sat on the couch where he used to nap very often after the exhaustion of his office work. Amira wasn't available at home and Richard was having a plate of luscious spaghetti with sausages for dinner. Joseph didn't speak a word and Richard maintained his silence too.

"Where were you all this time?" a rough voice questioned.

Joseph bucked up to see who it was and Amira stood crossing her hands on her stomach.

"I should question you but you are questioning me?" Joseph exclaimed.

"Your friends rang to me several times asking where you were, when I came home after college. I informed them that you didn't arrive home yet. They told me that you've misplaced your mobile at home and they are unable to get in touch with you. Even I had searched for it. But I didn't get it. Finally, I rang your number and a lady picked up the phone," Amira ended with a long breath.

"What the hell? A lady?" Joseph scratched his head in confusion.

"I am pretty sure that she must be having it," Amira replied.

"Who is she?"

"She never told me her history," Amira winked her eyes and pulled out her tongue.

Joseph gazed at her ridiculous reaction and sighed, "I don't know what's wrong. My mobile is missing since last night. I should have missed it at La Barista."

"Then why did you fabricate a fake story to your friends?" Amira disgruntled.

"Oh...I am sorry...I wasn't aware of anything. I forgot...Please understand, Amira," Joseph tried to explain.

"I hope you weren't intoxicated to forget everything. Anyway, I don't know who she is or her details. She said a 'hello' and when I inquired where you were, she didn't reply. She ended the call as well," Amira clarified further.

"Okay, Let's call her again," Joseph suggested.

He took Amira's mobile and dialled his number. The ring was going on, no one picked it up. He tried for the second time and he heard a golden voice over the mobile.

"Hello," the voice of the lady was too husky.

"Hello, it's Joseph. Can I know who are you?" Joseph hurried.

"Why do you want my details?" she sounded a bit rude.

"Oh...Okay...Cool... Anyway, I don't want to know about you. The mobile through which you are speaking to me is mine. Can I know when and how can I get it?" Joseph detailed his purpose.

"Oh...Are you the possessor of this mobile?"

"Yeah,"

"Then, reply to my question," She said steadily.

"Ehhh...Okay."

"Where did you leave your mobile?"

"At 'La Barista' on a dessert brown table," Joseph confirmed.

"Exactly right. You can get your mobile at Costa Coffee shop if you can reach here within half an hour," She said hastily.

"But, how is it possible? It takes around forty five minutes to reach there from my dwelling due to the traffic congestion. So, I am unable to...," the lady ended the call before Joseph had completed his sentence.

"Oh My God, she isn't ready to pay attention to anything. She is intricate," Joseph stuttered as he took his the key of his car and headed over to Costa Coffee Shop.

Joseph drove as quickly as possible. As he was a skilled driver, he managed the hectic road and reached 'Costa Coffee shop' within twenty five minutes. Only then, Joseph realized his huge blunder. He should have taken Amira's or Richard's mobile with him to give her a call because he neither knew her name nor her features. At least, if she had said the colour of her dress, he could have guessed her but she was inexorable. Joseph looked around, up and down. He was helpless. He felt as if everyone around fixed their eyes on him.

Suddenly, someone from behind called 'Joseph'. He whirled back to see who it was and it was she. Yes, that anonymous girl again.

"Joseph...? How do you know my name?" Joseph stammered.

"It's written on your forehead," She answered flatly and handed over his mobile.

"Oh...Is that you? Thank you....so much! Miss...Miss...?" Joseph stammered again.

"Elena...Elena Suzanne...," She said staring at him.

"Elena....Thank you so much! But how did you find me out?" Joseph was excited.

"The picture on the lock screen is yours, isn't it?" She raised her shaped dark eyebrows.

"That's smart. I was afraid of finding you out in the crowd. Thank God," Joseph snickered.

Elena did not give further reaction to what Joseph had said. It seemed that she didn't like to have any lengthy conversations with him. She turned her face away and scooted out of Costa.

"Elena, would you like to have a coffee with me?" Joseph insisted.

"No," Elena said.

"But I would like to, from the time I saw you at 'La Barista'," Joseph said in a cheerful tone.

Elena stopped for a moment and glared at Joseph. "Mr. Joseph, I don't like people who speak in a roundabout way. I hate that. Be frank or get the hell out of here," Elena growled.

Joseph glued his mouth for a second. He felt that she must be a rude girl but in a nice way. He loved that. A generous girl will always try to avoid an unknown man in such a way. She never gave space for him. He walked behind her, observing her and the night sky. She was shining like a pearl in the silvery moonlight night. The twinkling stars were chasing her. She walked as swiftly as she could and her hair moved slowly, back and forth, due to the cool breeze.

"Elena...," Joseph called her so softly.

She turned behind and looked at his eyes.

"You want me to be open-minded? That's fine. Elena...Let me tell you something that I really want to pour out before talking about the main subject. I feel that clouds are following you right now along with me. Don't you feel that? Look at the stars...It is flirting with you so much. Look! The next time I am going to shoot them right now for looking at your gorgeous features. Your face is glowing brighter than that of the shining moon, Oh My God. I think that nature is jealous of your beauty," Joseph whispered.

Before Joseph could reveal his love to her, the sound of a car horn nearly killed his ears. Joseph and Elena peered and a white Hatchback came at a high speed and parked at the other end of the street where both of them stood.

Elena crossed the road and opened the door of the car. "I still don't understand your intention. You better try poetry, at least you can become a great poet. Goodbye!" Elena hinted.

SIX

THAT WAS ANNIE!

It was getting too late and Joseph rushed home. Amira was waiting at the entrance for Joseph till late at night to inquire about his lost mobile. Joseph came home with a reddish blush on his face. His face was glowing unusually, Amira noticed. "Did you get your mobile?" Amira raised a question. "Yeah," Joseph replied in a single word and went back to his room. Amira raised her eyebrows and gave a long breath.

The next day morning, Joseph headed to the office as usual. He felt a bit awkward to meet his friends for what he had done yesterday. Max and Bob were seated in their cabins. Joseph said a 'Hello' while entering inside to which both of them didn't reply.

"I was in a tough dilemma yesterday. Hope you guys will try to understand. I prowled in search of my mobile like a street dog all the day," Joseph explained.

"We know, Amira notified us about it. My question is, why didn't you inform us before leaving the office yesterday? We stayed around half an hour looking for you in the car," Bob interrogated.

"Oh My God! I am sorry for the inconvenience caused by me. I was in a haste," Joseph apologised.

"That's fine anyway. Where did you leave your mobile?" Max inquired.

"At 'La Barista'...A genuine lady had taken it yesterday from one of the tables there. She handed it over to me at 'Costa Coffee Shop' last night."

Both of them listened to Joseph and kept quiet.

"How... is Annie's mom? Hope... she is doing...well?" Joseph questioned dubiously.

"Yes, she is doing well," Bob answered back.

"Can I know the name of the hospital?"

"Durdans Hospital," Max gave the answer.

Joseph was ransacked with guilt for not visiting Annie's mom the before day. Annie had been a generous friend of him for two years. His friends screwed up their friendship for a relationship. It hurt Joseph to the core of his heart. He never imagined Annie being his wife or soulmate. He started to maintain distance from Annie because he thought that his friends might misunderstand them and their friendship. But still, he needed to visit Annie's mom at least to comfort her.

Joseph was already running short of time. He wanted to visit Annie's mom, meet his love, Elena and reach home before 09:00 p.m. Joseph wasn't allowed to wander in the road at night as his Dad was strict regarding night outs. He drove as fast as he could to 'Durdans Hospital' from his office. He headed to the receptionist to inquire about the ward and the room number. Once he collected the information, he got into the lift and reached the room where Annie's mom was admitted.

"Can I enter inside?" Joseph was decent in asking permission.

"Oh Joseph, Please come inside," Annie welcomed him with a glow in her face.

Joseph entered and to his surprise Max, Bob and John were already present in the room. Three of them were staring at Joseph so weirdly.

"How is your mom doing now?" Joseph inquired.

"Much better than yesterday," Annie replied with a hard smile on her face.

"Don't worry. She will get well soon", Joseph comforted and continued, "And I am sorry for not answering your calls yesterday because….,"

"Yeah, Bob detailed everything just now. That's okay, Joseph…Unexpected things happen, which cannot be adjusted. We can't blame people for that because all of them are encountering various tough situations at different points in their life. It's by God's grace that John was able to help me on time," Annie replied in an easy-going way.

Joseph looked at John and thanked him. He felt that a pinch of jealousy had aroused into his heart but he didn't know the reason behind it.

Meanwhile, Joseph heard voices of two females that were getting closer to the room in which Annie's mom was admitted. One of the voices was much familiar to Joseph.

"Hey Annie, How are you doing?" the familiar voice questioned.

Joseph looked up to see who it was.

"Joseph, You are here," Amira was excited.

"Amira…How come you are here?" Joseph inquired uncertainly.

"This is Nancy, My friend," Amira pointed to the tall, frail girl who was standing next to her. "I came to visit her sick mother. Nancy, meet my brother Joseph."

"Hello," Nancy said in a soft tone to which Joseph replied the same 'Hello' in return.

"I never knew that Joseph was your brother," Annie said merrily looking at Amira.

"Do you know him already?" Amira questioned.

"Yeah, we work together," Joseph interrupted roughly.

"That's awesome. We are well known between each other but unknowingly. How's mom doing?" Amira conversed with Annie to which Annie gave her short replies.

While their conversations were going on, millions of thoughts started surrounding Joseph's mind. "When I asked Amira about her sister-in-law, she said that she must be similar to Nancy's sister. Nancy's sister means, it is Annie. Yeah, of course, Annie is easy-going, beautiful and intelligent as well. It seems like she will ask me to marry her if the track runs like this," Joseph feared for himself.

"Okay, I am leaving now," Joseph stood up.

"Wait...Wait...You are going home, aren't you?" Amira stood up too.

"No, I am going to meet one of my friends right now. You better go home now, before it gets too late, " Joseph ordered.

Amira nodded her head and Joseph said a 'bye' to everyone present in the room and walked out while Annie came running behind him.

"Thank you so much, Joseph," Annie said gladly.

"That's Okay. But why do you thank me for?"

"For visiting my mom, for comforting me and so on," Annie said so softly.

"I never did anything so greater than what John had done for you," Joseph ended and turned back to walk further.

"Joseph, Do you have any grudge against me?" Annie came to the point.

"Nothing like that. Why do you ask that?" Joseph asked in such a way that he is unaware of his recent behaviour.

"No, I feel that you are trying to maintain a huge gap between me and you. I can feel the difference in you. Do let me know If I had wronged you in any situation. I will apologise for it and I promise you that I will never repeat it," Annie fretted.

"OH MY GOD, Annie please try to understand. I have been trapped in a small issue. I am running a rat race to solve it as soon as possible. Don't ask me anything for now. Once everything is solved, I will let you know," Joseph pleaded and Annie remained quiet.

SEVEN
THE WAITRESS

Joseph drove into every street in search of Elena. He was compelled to do because the only detail he knew about her was Elena, her beautiful name. Weariness governed him after a hard search for her. He badly needed a short break to invigorate himself with a hot cup of coffee. So, he headed towards Costa Coffee Shop. Costa wasn't crowded at the time Joseph reached there. It seemed that a few couples were seated inside and most of the tables remained vacant. Joseph took over a seat and ordered a cup of coffee.

Within a few moments, Joseph was able to taste the caramel flavoured coffee in his tongue. He deliberately realized that the aches in his head is getting evacuated somewhere far away. He cupped the warm mug of coffee in his hand and looked up. Max and John were seated right opposite to him. Joseph rolled his eyes up and down wondering when they had arrived here.

"Why are you frowning at us?" Max asked.

"Frowning? Hun, not at all. I am scrutinizing," Joseph replied hilariously.

"Don't try to compete me in cracking crazy jokes, I bet you can never win over me," Max challenged Joseph.

"Anyway, what's wrong with you man? Your behaviour seems to be sophisticated since two days," Bob jotted out the difference in Joseph.

"Nothing is wrong with me. Yesterday was a nightmare for me only because of the missing mobile. That's all," Joseph made it simple.

"Is that all? Okay, That's fine. Then, it would be a great pleasure if you could order us a plate of British Chicken and Mushroom Toastie with two cups of hot Cinnamon Latte," Max grinned. Joseph scowled at Max for a considerable time and the waitress arrived at the table to note down the orders from the newly arrived customers, Max and Bob. Joseph did not take off his eyes from Max but he realized that the waitress is standing by the side of the table waiting for the order. "Two cups of Cinnamon Latte only...," Joseph stressed the word 'only' and symbolized the waitress with his index and middle finger. "I just ordered only for a caramel flavoured coffee but you crave for British Chicken and American Mushroom Toasties, Hun?" Joseph raised his voice from a low pitch to a higher pitch and took a glimpse at the waitress abruptly.

"I never added a word called American there," Max cried out.

Joseph did not respond. His heart paused for a moment. He observed the waitress so attentively. He couldn't believe in his eyes. The waitress was cutest Elena, dressed in a burgundy red T-shirt and a carbon black apron. She wore dark black jeans and a shoe similar to the colour of the jeans. Holding the menu in her hand, she pretended as if she never knew Joseph before.

"Is that all, Sir?" Elena asked humbly.

Joseph did not utter a single word because he drowned himself in astonishment.

"Yes Madam, that's all. He will nail me on the wall if I order anything further because he pays for it," Max ended with a wink.

Elena blushed and left the place to bring back the order to the table. And, Joseph never raised his head.

"She is so ravishing, isn't she?" Bob winked at Max.

"Yeah, but beauty doesn't matter because, in the end, we all lose our looks and all we have is our heart, a famous saying by Ann Curry," Max replied.

"We are the most fortunate ones if our better half possess a beautiful soul along with a beautiful appearance as well," Joseph said with full of hopes drooling over Elena's character.

"Well said, " Bob clapped his hands.

The Cinnamon latte arrived at the table with a strong aroma. Bob and Max sipped their latte while Joseph peered here and there, trying to catch a glimpse of Elena. Joseph expected that she would come back to collect the bill but she never came back. Another waiter had been appointed instead of her. Joseph, Bob and Max dispersed in various directions to their dwellings from Costa once their refreshments were over.

Joseph arrived home and went straight to his mind relaxing bedroom. He opened the windows and poked his head out. The bliss of the newly blossomed love made him float in high skies. He felt that he was falling for her deeper and deeper. 'There is no love like the first' and he reckoned it true. He preferred to think about Elena all the while consciously or subconsciously.

But the only matter which kicked his heart was 'Who is she?' The first time when he saw her, she was exactly looking like a fashion model and her style too proved it. When different luxurious cars came to pick her up, he even thought that she must most probably be a businesswoman or a billionaire's daughter. But when he saw her working at 'Costa' as a waitress, his assumptions became wrong. Elena wasn't a fashion model nor a businesswoman. And she was neither a billionaire's daughter. The truth is that she was a waitress at 'Costa'.

"How is it possible for her to own expensive luxurious cars? Oh no, it cannot be hers. But who is picking her up if her father isn't a Billionaire? If he is so, then Elena deserves to be a wealthy woman too," Joseph held his hands on his forehead realising that his head was about to break into pieces.

EIGHT

I LOVE YOU

After a long inquisition to himself, Joseph mumbled, "Whoever She is, she is mine," glaring at the crystal clear mirror, "I owe her."

It was on a bright Sunday morning, Joseph dressed up stylishly in a slim fit white shirt and blackish blue denim. He fixed his mind to meet Elena and express his feelings towards her on that following day. He was excited to the top of his mind and his heart shivered due to the acceleration of restlessness in his mind because of the unrequited love that was tormenting him every second.

"I am an introverted guy. How am I going to express my love today? Whenever my eyes scan her figure, my tongue automatically utters words that a poet uses in his poems which she hates very much," Joseph felt cowardly. He was uncertain if he could meet Elena as he was unaware of her programs for the day. His only hope was that God would give him a chance to express his desires to her as he wishes.

Joseph fetched the 'J' alphabet, stone embedded key of his car that was left at the butterscotch coloured tiny coffee table last night and headed further while his mobile rang. It was a call from Annie.

"Why is she calling now?" Joseph gaped as he answered the call.

"Hello, Joseph,"

"Hello, Annie, What's up?"

"Joe, I am very sorry to disturb you this early morning. My mom is getting discharged from the hospital today. I need your assistance to get her home. That is the reason why I phoned you. If you are swarmed with works do let me know. I can ask John if...," Joseph interrupted in between, "Oh no, I am not hectic as you think. Do wait, I'll be there within half an hour."

Annie ended the call and gave an affiliative smile at Max, "Joe will come here."

"Annie, did you see how my plan worked out so perfectly," Max said so proudly.

"It doesn't mean that he loves me if he agrees to come here," Annie talked rationally.

"Whether he loves you or not, you must express your love to him. The rest will have to be decided by him but, you have to accept and respect his decision," Max advised and continued, "Dear Annie, I hope he will never reject you. No man will get a girl better than you. Your personality is quite stunning. At the time when you told me about your unending love towards him, I was at the top of my head. You know he had lost his dear mom. He is bitterly yearning for so much love. I would be glad if you can satisfy him with whatever he wants in his life."

Annie remained quiet. Her only words were, "I am nervous."

Max left the hospital as soon as possible so that Joseph would not spot him out.

Joseph headed straight to 'Durdans Hospital'. He did not fail to remember his plan of the proposal to Elena. The cause for the change in his plan was that he just wanted to assist Annie as he could. He was guilty of not giving a helping hand to her, when her mom was faced with the very first heart attack. This time, he wanted to compensate for the guilt that he had in him.

"Annie, Is everything fine?" Joseph opened the door asking in a rough voice.

Annie stared at Joseph cluelessly for a long time. He looked so handsome in the white shirt and blackish blue denim. Annie's heart raced and her breathing accelerated. She felt like hugging him so tight. She was blushing unconsciously as well.

"Annie, What's wrong?" Joseph looked strangely.

"You are handsome," Annie mumbled.

"What?"

"Ahh... Nothing Joe, All the procedures are over. Let's go home," Annie replied.

Joseph took the huge luggage and held it in his grip. "I'll place it in the back of the car and come back," Joseph said so politely. His appearance was so cute and caring when he said that. Annie never asked him to carry the luggage, he did it without her order. He could have told Annie to do that but he didn't want a girl to drag it through the stairs or lift.

Joseph went out of the room and Annie came running behind him. She poked her head out of the room and observed him till he disappeared.

"Annie, I hope you have almost submitted your heart to him," Annie's mom inquired in a quite happy tone.

"Mummy...Ehhh...Nothing like that," Annie stepped back inside the room and rolled her eyes.

"I have been noticing you and your behaviours whenever he is present around. Don't lie, even I had passed the same stage in my life, the same thoughts and experiences," Annie's mom spoke in a more friendly manner. Annie realized that her mom too had experienced such kind of feelings during her youth which made her identify Annie's love today. As a mom, she never warned her not to fall in love with him nor avoid speaking to him, unlike other parents. Her only words were, "Do what is right for you because it is your life. You are going to live it. Whatever befalls, I assure you that I will stand by your side." Annie was so glad to hear that. Her mom's advice boosted her energy to the top. Annie had so many pillars in her life, who were supporting her. She felt it was a great blessing from God. The only desire she had in her heart was, to make Joseph hers.

Joseph came back to the room with a wheelchair. He came closer to Annie's mom and held her by his rigid arms while Annie supported him. His white shirt slightly drenched in sweat but still, he was keen on settling Annie's mom to the wheelchair. He pulled the wheelchair along the hospital corridor and to the lift. Annie didn't want to burden him anymore. She said him to take off and she kept her soft palms on the steel bar of the wheelchair to push it further but unfortunately, Joseph hadn't taken off his hands.

"I came here to assist you but whenever I see your mom, I remember mine. So, please take off your hands. I will do it myself," Joseph said.

Annie slowly took her hand from his hands reluctantly. She did not want to take it off but Joseph had told her to do so and she was helpless at that moment.

Annie and her mom got into the car and Joseph drove towards Annie's home. Once again, Annie started to tremble with fear. Her heartbeat was at a rate that was equal to the speed of the lightning. The time was getting closer and closer. Once Joseph drops them, he would go. Annie was supposed to propose to him before he leaves, that was an order from Max. Annie thought of postponing it to some other day because she didn't want to be in a rush.

They reached home in twenty minutes and Joseph accompanied Annie's mom to the bedroom. He laid Annie's mom comfortably on the bed.

"I hope everything is fine, May I leave now?" Joseph asked the permission.

"Are you in a haste, My dear son? Please stay for a hot cup of tea," Annie's mom requested.

Joseph did not refuse, he nodded his head once Annie's mom requested from him.

Annie ran to the kitchen and made a tea for him with much excitement. The water was boiling at 100° Celsius and millions of thoughts harboured Annie's mind. There is a saying that 'Good things should never be delayed.' The saying crisscrossed Annie's mind. Postponing certain things in life can make you lose them forever. "No, I am not ready to lose him. I can never bear that torment in my life. I will express my love to him today. No more hesitations," Annie made up her mind bravely.

Joseph was seated in the living room because he didn't want to disturb Annie's mom. Annie came towards Joseph and handed him the pure ivory coloured mug with creamy hot tea. Annie cleared her throat while Joseph started sipping the tea.

"Joe," Annie called softly.

Joseph looked up at her face.

"I LOVE YOU," said Annie deeply from the bottom of her heart.

"What?" Joseph questioned while his eyes were wide open.

"I am sure you heard me," Annie replied.

Joseph looked down.

"Yes, for two years my heart was beating by your name. The love I had for you has grown up so much and I am unable to hide it further," Annie explained.

Joseph gave a wounded look at Annie. He never expected this from her. What had he done to make her fall in love with him so deeply, he wasn't aware of it. But the only thing that he wanted to tell was a 'goodbye' to Annie without hurting her.

Annie glued her eyes on him for a long time. Her heart was battering with excitement and fear. A pin drop of silence prevailed in the living room.

"I am very sorry to hurt you. I am already in love with another girl," Joseph said sharply.

Annie was literally blown by the response that she got from him. The door swung slightly open about which Annie and Joseph were unaware of. Tears were rebelling with Annie's eyes trying to gush out. She dominated it hardly, sitting like a statue carved out of cement.

"I apologise if I had behaved in such a way to make you fall in love with me. Goodbye!" Joseph got up from the green couch on which he was seated and left the place as soon as possible. Annie watched Joseph till he disappeared. She burst into uncontrollable tears which flooded in her eyes when Joseph was seated in front of her. Someone from behind tapped her shoulders so softly. Annie turned back and it was her mom. She draped her tears and tried to dominate her sobs again.

"Cry, cry as much as you can. Let the dense of worries evacuate your heart, you will feel relaxed. If it isn't written for you, it isn't. I hope you will try to get out of the heartbreak very soon," Annie's mom advised.

NINE

THE TRUTH BEHIND HER

Joseph went home with a heart disturbed by uncommon emotions. Annie's proposal bothered him a lot. The way tears blocked her eyes, her reaction when he told her that he was already in an affair with another girl, nearly tormented his heart. He thought that he should put an end to all kinds of stuff that was disturbing him.

"I should find Elena today," he stood up, "I should pour out my feelings to her, ask her opinion that she holds in her heart," Joseph rushed out like a gust of wind. He loafed on the paved roads and clumsy streets like a stray dog. He was unable to find her anywhere in the city. His heart was overloaded with confusion and millions of questions provoked in his mind.

"Where is she?"

"Does she ever like me or not?"

"Will she accept my love or reject me just like the way how I rejected Annie?" Joseph muttered to himself like an insane. He crossed past the bus stand which was located right opposite La Barista. Suddenly, he caught a glimpse at it. A girl, who sounded like Elena, dressed in a sky blue cotton dress was conversing over the phone. He stopped his car and had a swift walk towards her. He intended to verify if it was Elena or had he mistaken her for someone else. He came closer and closer to her. Yes, it was Elena. Once she saw Joseph approaching her, she ended the call and swerved to the other side with a look of annoyance on her face.

"Elena," Joseph called out.

She turned her head back and then front. She walked further not willing to speak to him.

"Elena, please stop. I hope you aren't angry with me, are you?" Joseph yelled.

Elena stopped and veered her whole body this time.

"What's your problem? Why are you following me like a pet dog, Hun?" Elena asked in a rage.

"Yes, I am your pet dog, Elena Suzanne, I am your pet dog," Joseph repeated twice.

Elena gritted her teeth and tightened her fists.

"I am here to tell you something. I know you hate people who speak indirectly. I will come to the point right now. The first time I saw you, I think, I had fallen, fallen in love with you. From that day onwards, I have been searching for you like an idiot, idiot means idiot. I have become an insomniac in the recent past, thinking of you all night. Just like the clouds slid past the pale moon, the memories of you keeps on sliding across my heart. What's further to say? I need you badly throughout my life," Joseph shifted his eyes towards her with utmost love.

Elena rubbed her forehead wearily, chortled and shook her head, "Can you please define your love? I mean the type of love that you have for me?"

"Of course, I love you, want to get married to you, have kids through you and finally live the rest of my life with you, beloved Elena," Joseph spread both of his hands with a gesture depicting what more.

"Ohhh...That type of love?" Elena raised her thickly shaped brows.

"Yeah, Can I know what type of love that you expected?" Joseph questioned.

"Yeah, you will get to know about it in a while. I don't offer the type of love that you want. What I can after all offer you is Lust, only lust. Because I am a prostitute. An escort who isn't visible to the public eye," Elena revealed.

"You better stop the ridiculous jokes that you are cracking now. Whatever it is, tell it to my face and please don't lie," Joseph raised his manly voice.

"I am not joking, Mr. Joseph. I promise on the bible. I am a prostitute, who is satisfying the needs of various rich men in the city. They pay 400$ to 600$ per time. If you can afford, book a private room and let me know. One more condition to be applied, you are supposed to send a car to pick me, just to hide me from the eyes of people. That's all," Elena detailed her job as a prostitute.

Joseph's heart hammered into pieces. Tears were leaking down in the corner of his eyes. He felt that his desires about her were getting drifted in different paths. Whom he had thought would be his future love was a call girl, after all, a sex worker as she had promised in the Bible, roaming around like a virgin in the eyes of people. He had judged a book by its cover but the fluttering dirty pages inside it remained a mystery for him. The different coloured luxurious cars which he saw were the cars of those rich men that was sent to pick her up as per her deal. Her style, hard smile, haute couture designer gowns, dark red moisturising lipstick and a shapely maintained body was only to grab the attention of those wealthy men.

"One more clarification please, Can I know why do you want to work as a waitress at a coffee shop while you have all the amenities to enjoy your life to the best?" Joseph verified.

"I already told you that I am an unseen woman of the streets in the public point of view. I work at 'Costa' for the world. My wholehearted profession is this," Elena detailed.

"What made you fall into this trap, Is it poverty or did anyone forcibly..."

"That's enough, you don't deserve to know about my personal life. Get it straight, if you can afford my rate, call," she held out a card in which her mobile number was written, "if not, buzz off somewhere instead of hanging in the edge of my tail everywhere," Elena hollered.

Joseph remained silent. Yes, he did not have any rights over her, to poke his head into her personal life. All that he could do was, sit and watch at the darkening sky in which the cauliflower-shaped smoky grey clouds moved like a tortoise.

TEN

FAKE

That evening, Annie's phone rang in a silent mood. It was a phone call from Max. Annie gazed at her phone and answered the call.

"Hello,"

"Hello, Max, What's up?"

"I have been ringing to you for an hour but you seem not to respond to any of my calls. What's up? Have you proposed to him?" Max asked excitingly.

"Yeah," Annie whimpered quietly.

"Oh wow," Max jumped out with joy.

"You never told me that he is already in love with another girl. Did you want me to get embarrassed in front of him?" Annie sobbed.

"What? What do you mean? Joseph in love? From when was that? I neither knew about it nor he told me?" Max rushed in his questions.

"I couldn't raise an inquiry about the history of his love, I am sorry to say that I am unaware of the date and time on which he fell in love with that lucky girl. All that I know is, he is in love with a girl. That's all he told me. He said it to me as a reason for rejecting my love," Annie freaked out.

Max was shocked for a moment. His face turned dull in despair. Why did Joseph want to hide his love to him? Not only to him, even Bob and John must be unaware of it. If he had known about Joseph's affair, he wouldn't have forced Annie to propose to him.

"Everything has gone over the head now. I apologise for what I had done to you," Max said in distress.

Annie didn't have words to speak. She bit her lips and tightened her face in sorrow.

Joseph kept on observing the twinkling tiny stars and the pale crescent shone like a silvery claw in the night sky. The street lights were dim and he could hear the occasional barks of the far-away dogs breaking the silence of the night. He was seated on the wooden bench the whole night, thinking of the events that had occurred chronologically. Annie's proposal, his hard search for Elena throughout the tiresome day, his proposal and finally, the truth behind her. The temperature decreased, it was extremely cold and foggy. Nothing was visible clearly. His hands were numb. The collapse in his heart nearly ignored the coldest atmosphere. He slowly closed his eyes and leaned on the bench. Subsequently, he fell asleep without his mere knowledge.

The sun rose early morning, the brightest rays from it stroke Joseph's face and pierced through his eyes which made him wake up from his sleep squinting his eyes. It was still frigid, the environment was dull and dismal as well. Mists and fog were covered all over, he could hear the sound of the wind whipping through the trees, groaning and creaking like an old chair. He was almost shivering. He unsteadily stood up and got into his car. He fished inside his pocket for the key and headed home.

He walked shakily into the hall, his legs were stiff. "There comes Joseph," Amira yelled cheerfully.

Joseph raised his head and scrutinized. Max, John and Bob were seated in the low seated peach sofa and Richard was sitting on the grey couch scowling at him, his arms and legs crossed. John rushed towards him noticing the changes that his body had endured. He was pale and frail. He stumbled a lot.

"What has gone wrong, Joseph? Where were you last night? We have been roaming in the streets like police dogs, searching for you," John inquired trembling with fear.

"Oh, I think I had overloaded your brains with tensions and terrible thoughts. Losing your one night's sleep would have been a horrible day for you guys. I apologise," Joseph was still shaky in his voice.

"That's nothing for us. Do tell me, where were you?" Bob came in between John and Joseph.

"Err...I went to St.Sebastine Church yesterday evening for prayers and I was walking...Err...over the bridge near St.Sebastine Church. I hope you know that...Err...St.Sebastine, right? I suddenly fell unconscious there...When I woke up early morning...Err... I acknowledged that I was laying on the wooden planks of the bridge," Joseph spoke like an intoxicated drunkard.

Every one of them present there knew that it was a bitter story fabricated by Joseph. His illustration seemed completely bogus and unbelievable. First of all, the bridge was located two kilometres away from St.Sebastine Church. Joseph couldn't have fallen unconscious at the church and laid on the wooden bridge that was two kilometres away from the church. It was nearly impossible. Any nincompoop will never trust his words. There will be many people passing by the streets. If he had truly fallen on the bridge unconsciously, why didn't those people help him to reach home? Their inner minds questioned intensely but they remained calm.

"Just leave it. Thank God, He is safe. You go and rest for a while," John spouted his words before anyone questioned Joseph about the loopholes in his lies.

All of them rolled up their eyes, stumbling to inquire Joseph but John gave no space for it. John knew Joseph was lying. But he understood that Joseph was broken as well. John fixed an alarm in his mind to inquire the truth privately from him.

Joseph left the living room and infiltrated into his mind comforting bedroom. The boys shattered in various directions to their residences to have a rest. Richard and Amira sat wondering what might have gone wrong with Joseph.

Richard lengthened his face with a deep sigh, "If Regina was alive today, she wouldn't have let this happen." Amira sensed the suffering that her father had endured all this period without his wife.

"What can we do? It's all written in our fate," Amira said in desperation.

ELEVEN
ISOLATION

Joseph never preferred to get out of his room on that day. Early morning coffee; toasted crusty sandwiches for breakfast; fried rice for lunch and Mushroom filled oily pasta for dinner was brought by Amira to his room. Richard never planned of poking into Joseph's room as he was at the top of his temper.

The next day morning, John paid a call to Joseph's house. They both sat inside the room, keeping the doors shut. "What's wrong, Joe?" John inquired.

"Nothing," Joseph retorted simply, not ready to speak.

"I know about the entire scene that had happened yesterday. Max told me. Who is that girl?"

"Which girl?" Joseph raised his eyebrows.

"I am discussing about the girl whom you love... We got to know about your hidden love just because of Annie," John replied frankly.

"Oh...she did publicized my secrets, didn't she? Is that what she calls true love?" Joseph growled.

"My God, She never disclosed anything deliberately. Max knew that Annie was on a serious affair with you, everyone of us knew about it except you. That was the reason why

Max spoke in such a way on your birthday. Hope you can remember? He did that to dig out what resided in your heart about Annie. He was the one who had compelled Annie to express her love to you as well. When everything went wrong, Annie was obliged to give an account of the reason for your rejection. She thought that we already knew about your love. Moreover, she misunderstood that Max had forced just to embarrass her in front of you. But we never knew, you did not introduce your angel to us," John regretted.

"Nothing like that," Joseph pivoted his head.

"What? Look, Joe. Love is like Sunshine, you cannot hide it. Though you do, the rays will penetrate through any hole."

"Nothing means nothing, why don't you understand? I can't clarify further," Joseph said disgruntled.

John realized that Joseph wasn't willing to share any of his secrets with him. He got up at a speed that was as fast as the lightning, rushed out of the room and slammed the door shut again.

"Am I behaving like a psychopath or what? He said 'your angel.' How would he react if he gets to know that she is a woman of the streets or a woman of so many wealthy men? What is going to be my decision regarding her? What will happen if I bring a call girl into my house? Amira will have to become a nun at the end. Yes, a nun. Because no one will accept her as a daughter-in-law when her sister-in-law at home was a prostitute before. They might think that Amira too possesses a ruined character. But still, Elena is working as a secret prostitute. Unless I tell about it, none of them will know about it," an idea emerged in Joseph's mind.

He had a short glimpse at the card given by Elena, which he held in his left hand. He dialled her number on the mobile which he held in his right. In two short rings, Elena answered the call.

"Who is this?" Her first words weren't 'Hello,' just like others would say. Elena was a lady who was always up to the point.

"I am Joseph," he spoke politely.

"Oh, what's the matter?"

"I can pay you 500$ per night. I'll book a room at a four-star hotel and share the location with you. Be present at 07:00 p.m.," Joseph said in a shivering tone.

"Okay, I'll be there," Elena replied in a single sentence.

Drops of sweat were rolling down his face, his heart was heavy, palms and feet were frozen. He laid on his bed, thinking intensely. He couldn't even close his eyes. Disturbance in the heart, mind harboured with emotional strains did not let him fall asleep that night. He woke up from the bed and had aimless walks throughout the night.

The sun rose to start a fresh day. Joseph got ready earlier than usual and headed to the office. Annie arrived at the office before him. When Joseph passed the main door, Annie gazed at his dull face and opened her mouth to say a 'Hello' but he glanced and went straight to his cabin without a word. Annie's face shrank and her heart shattered further into pieces due to his ignorance. He had been a good friend of hers. Yes, of course, she proposed to him out of love and he rejected her. That was over. Why did he want to encounter her like a foe? She never did anything bad to him. Her biggest fault was her love for him. Annie grieved from her heart but she never revealed it to anyone.

Joseph neither had any conversations with his friends nor they had any chatting with him. He did not prefer to join them for a lunch break as well which they always enjoyed together. Annie worried a lot about the separateness between him and his friends. She guessed that she was the cause for Joseph's isolation. She yearned to compel Joseph to have lunch with them. But, whenever she looked into his dark frowning eyes, she was afraid that he might freak out at her. This made her, keep her tongue controlled.

TWELVE

NOT FOR PLEASURE

Joseph drove faster than usual to Roxby four-star hotel. The hotel was located three kilometres outside the city. He parked his car in the backyard of the hotel in such a way that no one could recognize or spot out that it was his car.

It was one of the most luxurious hotels with modern facilities including a swimming pool, tennis court, gym etc. Joseph didn't wait to see the interior design of the hotel. He had a short conversation with the receptionist and booked a room there. He made the payment and obtained the room key. After a glance at it, he shared the location with Elena.

Joseph headed to the room. He lacked time to raise his head and examine the hotel's adornments. He opened the door of his room. It was a single bedded bedroom with a dual inverter A/C, glued on the mirror textured wall. The room was luxurious with contemporary and fine murky wood details juxtaposed against painted images of stunning nature. Snowy white marbles glistened in the light. Sublime details appeared in flashes of gold. The wonderful bed linen was white on white. The fragrance of the fresh roses that remained in the clear glass vase reached Joseph's nose while Elena opened the door.

"Welcome, beloved Elena," Joseph snatched a rose from the vase and handed it over to her kneeling.

There was a glossy smile on her face which Joseph hadn't noticed before. She was extraordinary in the magenta coloured flattering frock and open wavy hair. Her lips were shaded with dark pink lipstick and her eyebrows were well-shaped this time. Joseph almost melted in his dream world.

Elena slowly approached him and hugged him tightly. Her fingers gently rubbed his body and she kissed his neck. Her aroma was arousing him but he controlled. Elena was breathing fast in ecstasy. Finally, She pushed him on the bed and laid next to him. She gently ran her index finger from his forehead, nose, neck and then the collar bone. The next moment, she unbuttoned his shirt, she brought her lips closer to his to get it locked. Suddenly, Joseph pushed her a bit, went closer to the dresser and held the edge of it.

"What happened? Am I not pleasing you?" Elena got up from the bed.

"Is this the way you treat all your customers?" Joseph grumbled.

"Yes, of course, I get paid for the level of satisfaction that I grant them," Elena retorted.

"Don't you feel ashamed to sleep with every man on this earth," Joseph groaned.

"What the hell? You called me to have pleasure but now you are embarrassing me," Elena hollered in a low pitched tone.

"I never called you to have pleasure with you. You never gave time for me. That was the only reason why I booked a room here, to speak to you in person. I came here to beg you to leave this escort business. I came here to beg you to be my wife, only my wife. I will never reveal your past to anyone. I love you so much, dear. I assure you, I will safeguard your dignity," Joseph pleaded like a toddler.

"Damn, please stop this shit... I would have never come here if I had known about your treacherous intention. You are going to safeguard my dignity? Hun? Which nail can you remove here with dignity? Money, money matters a lot here, not dignity," Elena growled raising her index finger towards Joseph.

Elena's words were nearly tattering Joseph's heart. She needed wealth. She thinks that currency can make anything happen. That was her world. She wanted to live in a world filled with luxurious apartments, Diamonds and gems, expensive cars and so on. She never wanted love. Love was the only thing that she hated the most.

Joseph leaned on the dresser and put his head down. He thought deeper, deeper than the depth of the oceans.

The knock on the door disturbed the silence in the room. Joseph threw a look at Elena, walked towards the door and opened it while Elena hid behind him.

There stood a tall, broad-shouldered man with a rigorous look in his eyes. It took a minute for Joseph to realize who he was. A piece of laminated card held the words, Mr. Stalin David, Deputy Commissioner of police. Joseph gazed at him while David examined him and Elena, multiple times.

"What's happening here?" David investigated.

"Eh...Nothing sir, we were... having a conversation," Joseph stammered.

"Oh, you booked a room to have conversations. I couldn't hear any of your conversations. I knew the room was dipped in silence when I came here. Tell me the truth, if not you will be hanged," David threatened.

"Sir, I pledge we were talking...," Joseph persuaded.

"Get the hell out of here. You were sleeping with her, weren't you? Brothel in a four-star hotel, Hun? Many families come here with kids, teenage boys and girls, to enjoy their leisure but people like you cause a nuisance to them. I didn't come here accidentally. The officers here informed me about the unusual behaviours of you both. Come, Come along with me to the police station now," David freaked out.

Joseph tried to convince David but David wasn't prepared to listen to anything that Joseph had explained to him. Elena's face was expressionless like a pure white paper. She continuously frowned at Joseph. Already she was in a temper and this incident poured oil into burning fuel.

They reached the police station within an hour. David made them be seated on a stool made with steel, that was placed in a corner of the police station.

"Now phone, phone your parents, ask them to come here. Let's see what sort of rapport you both have. Husband and wife? Lovers? or any other wrong type of relationships? I shall leave you after I had taken the wordings from them. Unless I am not prepared to trust both of you," David ordered.

Joseph glimpsed at Elena and she did the same too. Elena never pleaded from David to leave them just like Joseph had pleaded from David. She remained speechless, her stillness was in such a way that she accepted what David had meant was true. Within a moment, Elena fetched out her mobile from her tiny pink handbag, dialled a number fast and rang someone. She conversed in a very low husky voice and ended the call. Though she was seated so close to Joseph, he was unable to hear what she communicated.

Joseph had no idea to phone anyone. He was scared of losing his self-respect which he had gathered for ages.

Unfortunately, an office staff of Joseph, named Erick, visited the police station to file a missing case. He spotted out Joseph quickly from the outside through the long grilled window but Joseph did not notice Erick. Joseph was seated in such a way that his entire body was bent, fingers of both the palms twisted and elbows were supported on his knees.

"What's wrong with him, Sir?" Erick questioned from the constable near him.

"He got caught with a prostitute in a four-star hotel room," the constable said secretly in a low pitch.

Erick blinked his eyes, "With a prostitute? What the hell? I don't trust it. He is a golden boy."

"Look at her, she must be deadly on the bed. If a guy meets up with a lady like her, his golden heart acquires the possibility to turn into a rusted iron one," the constable winked.

Erick leaned front and poked his head to have a look at Elena. He raised his brows and bit his lips.

"Oh My God, I can't believe this. Anyway let's keep it away, I came here to file a missing case," Erick proceeded further.

A dark black, shiny surfaced jeep entered the territory of the police station at a high speed. Two men dressed in black and white office outfits got out of the car along with a medium height, fat man. He had a big belly and a thick beard. He was dressed in a grey coat and suit. His sight never fixed on the people around, except for Elena and David. The man approached David personally, spoke in a very low voice in such a way that no one around could hear them. He handed over a peach coloured envelope to David that was gladly accepted by him with a grin on his face. The man left the police station as immediately as possible.

"You can go now, Miss. Jenny," David said.

Joseph peered around to see who Jenny was but David's eyes were on Elena. Elena stood up, looked at Joseph's face arrogantly and growled, "Never ever come behind boot licking behind me."

Joseph's brain wasn't functioning at all. He couldn't believe what was happening around him. But, Joseph was pretty sure that David was bribed by that man. That fat man who entered the police station with so many build-ups must be a politician. Yes, Joseph was able to guess it out from his belly itself. The question that nailed Joseph's brain was, why should David address Elena as Jenny? He thought and his head was burning further.

"Damn it, she had played a fraud game with me. Not only myself, the entire crowd is being cheated by her. Her name is neither Elena nor Jenny. She is anonymous. She utters different names to different people so that her profession and identity could be hidden. What a shit she is? Beauty isn't a matter but the character is. Such a cheap character she possesses," Joseph thought, seated in the same posture how Erick had seen him.

Annie stood in front of him the next moment, Joseph raised his head. Max was with her. Joseph enlarged his eyes and put his head down in shame.

What happened, Joe? What's wrong? Erick rang Max when we were at John's flat and detailed the matter. I couldn't believe this could have happened," Annie said standing in front of Joseph but not looking at his face.

Joseph did not give a single response to her question, he remained tight-lipped as if Annie was cross-examining someone else. Annie got disheartened by his silence but Max burst out, "Stop it Annie, stop caressing for this bastard. A dump will spoil the entire city and he did prove that. I knew he is committing a big mistake, I understood from the behaviours he possessed within the last few days but I never thought up that he would fall into the trap of a prostitute and go behind her to..."

Annie slapped Max before he could utter the next word and a pin drop silence prevailed.

"Don't speak like a crazy man, Max. Even if the whole world had gathered here to spy on him, I am not going to trust any of them. I know him, I know him a lot. His personality is equal to a gem. Ask your apologies to him and I am going to speak to the Deputy Commissioner right now."

Joseph was stunned at Annie's speech. He never assumed that she would come here with Max. He rejected her, hurt her, but she stood for him at his tough time. Normally a young, unmarried girl doesn't enter the police stations for such kind of cases but she did. Society will create fairy tales about a girl who goes to the police stations. She never concerned about them. Everything she did was for him, he realized. Her love was true and a hundred per cent pure. Love, care and trust were the three important elements in a healthy relationship and Annie possessed them.

"The Deputy Commissioner to whom Annie has gone to speak is not a good man. He will eat her up," Joseph rushed into D.C's room.

"Excuse me sir," Joseph asked the consent from David.

Annie and D.C were already discussing while Joseph interrupted. Annie's face was desolate and David said, "Okay, you can leave now on one condition. You should settle the amount that you have promised me."

Annie nodded and jerked her head symbolically to Joseph asking him to leave the room. Within the next ten minutes, they were seated in the car.

"Why did you agree to bribe him?" Joseph grumbled.

"Because there was no way. Mr. David said that he cannot leave you at the requests of any person except your parents. He also had a talk saying that he would drag the case to the court. Just imagine what would happen if uncle Richard gets to know about this. Moreover, you will lose your dignity if it goes to the court. That is the only reason why I agreed."

"How much?" Joseph inquired.

"I am the one who agreed and I will pay for it," Annie's answer was like a bullet.

The car stopped at the Roxby four-star hotel. "My Dear Friend, please find your car that you treasured here a few hours ago and drive home safe instead of sleeping here and there. We can't be always searching for you. We will meet you tomorrow," Max hinted to which Annie chuckled.

Joseph glared at Annie and said, "Okay bye, Annie and Max. Thank you so much! Catch you tomorrow." Annie too waved a 'bye' in return.

Joseph felt that his heart was a truck which carried the dirty garbage of the entire city. He was ashamed of denying the authentic love of Annie. And the most embarrassing among all was, he had a rat race behind the bogus girl who's identity was completely a fabricated tale. What he had on her was infatuation or lust but not pure love, he realized. The Love that arises from the character is much stronger and long-lasting than the love that arises from the external beauty.

"I am the biggest ignoramus in the world," Joseph held his palms on his head realizing is stupidity.

She is just a nightmare to me, that's all," Joseph mumbled.

THIRTEEN

CAR CRASH

Joseph found his car in the backyard of Roxby four-star hotel where he had left it before. He drove home fast and entered his room. He bathed and fragranced himself. Amira brought the dinner, a hot plate of mushroom pasta with oyster sauce. Amira sat glaring at Joseph until he finished eating. Joseph ate to fill his stomach and settled his hunger to a limit.

"Dad is angry with you," Amira said.

"I know," Joseph responded.

"You know and you are repeating the same...,"

"I will put an end to all, I assure you," Joseph ensured.

"End to all means?"

"My late night arrivals that I am having from recent days," Joseph confessed.

Amira did not speak further, because she trusted her brother completely. She left the room silently with the empty plate. Joseph hopefully promised her because he didn't have the intention of going in search of that lady, the woman of the streets. He planned on amending his mistakes and bringing his life back to regular.

He glanced at the picture of his mom which hung in a frame on the wall opposite his bed. He came nearer to the frame and repented for what he had done. The cool breeze from the open window blew on his face. He perceived that it was a blessing from his mom and felt refreshed. Burden decreased as he observed the night sky, the twinkling tiny luminous stars and the smiling pale white moon. He remembered Annie and blushes entered his lips. Abruptly, he remembered the gift that Annie had presented him on his birthday. His heart wrenched when he recalled the way how he threw it carelessly behind his bed without even unwrapping it. He hunted for it behind the bed like a wild lion. Finally, he got it in his hand, dusty covered. He cleaned and unwrapped it. In it, he found a silver ring embedded with a red heart-shaped sapphire stone. He examined it with love and fitted it snugly in his finger. His heart cooled down as he walked backwards and fell on his bed, thinking about her. Annie resembled his mom. He felt cared for when being around her, just the way when Regina was around him. He couldn't wait until morning to see her friendly, smiling face. His heart was impatient.

"Please listen to me, I can't visit her now nor call her. What would she think of me if I do, a flirty person or a fool? Whatever she thinks, let her. I am going to phone her right now," He had a kind battle with his heart.

Within two rings, Annie picked up the phone. "Hello," she said in a silvery voice.

"Hello...Hem...Ohm....," Joseph cleared his throat further and further.

"Yeah, What's up, Joe? Hope you have reached home?"

"Yes, just half an hour ago. What about you?"

"Just now I dropped Max at his flat. I am driving home now," Annie replied.

"Okay, go home safe," Joseph said in a caring tone.

"Okay sure, bye, see you."

Joseph's face flickered so brightly after the conversation. His heartbeat accelerated as he closed his eyes. He felt that his mind was pure and peaceful. He was almost floating in the world of colourful dreams. Gradually he fell into a deep sleep.

Joseph's phone rang a couple of times at the midnight. Abruptly, he broke from his sleep and answered the call as it was a phone call from Annie. "Hello, Annie where are you?"

"Hello, I am not Annie," a different voice spoke on the opposite side.

"This girl met with an accident twenty minutes ago. She was bleeding with severe injuries. I admitted her to the nearby hospital," the opposite voice detailed.

"What? Accident...My Annie. You mean my Annie. Did she meet with an accident? You are joking right?" Joseph shuddered in fear.

"Sir, please try to understand. I am not kidding. I don't know if her name is Annie. When I checked her recent calls, she had spoken with you just before the accident had occurred. Please do arrive at 'Wilson Hospital', the treatment is going on," the girl ended the call.

Joseph rushed with his reddened eyes to the hospital. His heart throbbed in fear. He was afraid of losing her in his life. He drove as fast as he could while tears flooded his eyes. He reached the hospital within ten minutes and found out Annie's room number.

He wasn't allowed inside. The girl who called him, stood by the side. She comforted him with a few words, handed over Annie's peach soft handbag and left the place. Joseph was seated alone. He never phoned anyone. Max, Bob, John or Annie's family, none of them. Annie's phone rang several times, Joseph did not answer even one. Those phone calls were from Annie's mom.

"What would I say to her? Your daughter met with an accident or your daughter is rebelling with death," Joseph stumbled.

While the ringtones of Annie's mobile were tearing his ears, Joseph fished inside Annie's tiny handbag. It contained an identity card of Annie, a few dollars and a small photo of himself. Joseph scrutinized at his picture for a long time trying to remember when it was shot. It was during an office function that was held a year ago. From then, Annie was possessing it. Joseph could not reminisce who shot it.

Meanwhile, the doctor exited the ICU and rushed out to treat another patient. Joseph hindered the doctor's way and questioned him about Annie's condition.

"She is in a critical condition and I am unable to predict anything at the moment. Pray your God. But one thing, the blunt force trauma in the car accident against her head would cause blindness because the delicate optic nerves are severely damaged...," the doctor ended with a sigh.

Joseph was shocked, His heart ached like hell.

"Should this happen to her, for her kind heart?" Joseph shrieked.

Max rang Joseph and he attended the call.

"Joe, I am sorry to disturb you at this midnight. Annie's mom phoned me saying that Annie hasn't reached home yet. She dropped me and headed straight to her home but...I don't know. I was said that Annie didn't answer her calls. I am afraid that something is wrong," Max detailed while Joseph remained controlling his tears on his explanations.

"Joe, are you there?"

Joseph burst out, his cheeks reddened and tears wetted the beard.

"Joe, What happened?"

"Annie met with an accident. She is in critical condition at 'Wilson Hospital'. Please come here immediately with Bob and John. Don't inform her mom, I beg," Joseph ended the call crying.

Max, Bob and John reached immediately within a few minutes. Max saw Joseph seated in the corridor, dull faced with continuous tears. Max held Joseph's shoulders and comforted him. Bob and John stood by the side.

"How is she now?" John questioned.

"She is still critical but the worst thing is that she lost her eyesight," Joseph said.

"Oh my God, what are you saying? I feel so pity for Annie and her family. She is the one who earns for her family. What will happen to her entire family if she had lost her eyesight? May God heal her soon," John prayed for her.

"Nothing will happen to Annie or her family. I am there for her and God will cure her as soon as possible," Joseph said confidently and left to the church.

Meanwhile, Bob, Max and John stayed at the hospital, waiting for the doctor's words regarding Annie's health condition. Annie's mom kept on phoning Max and he lied the whole night telling her that they were searching for Annie.

FOURTEEN

GIVE ME A SECOND CHANCE

The next morning, the doctor informed that Annie had passed the fence of danger. Max, Bob and John were overjoyed. Bob pulled out his mobile to inform Joseph but he had already arrived at the hospital. Joseph's heart cooled down when he heard that Annie was safe. He took permission from the doctor and entered the room. Annie was lying on the bed like an angel. Patches here and there. He could easily observe her respiratory movements. He came closer and closer to her. He took a seat and slowly held her fair fragile fingers. Her eyelids dwindled and her lips moved as he observed her so carefully.

Annie's mom was informed and she arrived at the hospital with Nancy. Their heart shattered into pieces when they were told about Annie's eyesight but they contented their hearts saying that God saved her life.

Two days later, Annie moved towards a better condition. She was able to speak and sit in the wheelchair. But she never fussed so much when she was told about the loss of her sight. Pearl-like tears flowed from her eyes and she said, "God had wanted it, so he took hold of it." Everyone was amazed including Joseph. So much courage and bravery she had in her life which most of the women lacked.

A week passed and the doctor said that Annie could be discharged from the hospital. Annie's mom and Nancy had made all the arrangements when Joseph and Max came. Joseph winked his eyes and Max enunciated, "Aunty, you and Nancy can come with me in my car. I shall drop you at your house."

"Then what about Annie? She needs our help," Nancy interrupted.

"She doesn't need any of your help. She will come with Joseph," Max said.

"But,"

"But and Nut, Come with me, little broomstick," Max mumbled to Nancy.

Annie's mom and Nancy left the room with Max, rolling their eyes up and down. Annie was seated reactionless, unable to realize what was going on. Joseph pushed the wheelchair on which Annie was seated and went downstairs.

"Where are mom and Nancy?" Annie hardly spoke.

"They had gone home with Max."

"Why is it? All of us could go in the same car, couldn't we?"

"Yes, we could. But all of us aren't going to the same location," Joseph blushed.

"What? Where are we going to? My home, right?" Annie's face shrank in doubt.

"Yes home, but not your home," Joseph twisted his talks.

"Then whose home?"

"Wait and see," Joseph maintained suspense.

Joseph pushed the wheelchair until he reached his car. He carried Annie and made her sit comfortably in the front seat of the car. He folded the wheelchair and kept it behind the car and drove straight to the desired location. The car went up the hills and passed so many boundaries. Annie could feel that Joseph was driving to a fascinating location. Ultimately, after a long drive, Joseph stopped at the peak of a mountain.

He opened the door and supported Annie to get out of the car. He made her seated on a wooden bench that was fixed just below a tall oak tree with thick brownish bark. A vast silence dominated the area. The place itself was isolated and lifeless, without movement. The crisp autumn wind whipped through Annie's scarf and past her cheeks. She took a deep breath and felt the brisk air fill her lungs.

"Joe, I am glad that you took me to a spectacular place like this. Though nothing is visible to my eyes, I can feel everything around."

"I know...That is the only reason why I brought you here."

"But, my eyes are yearning to see this picturesque scenery," Annie's face shrank.

Joseph sat on his knees right opposite Annie. "Don't worry, Baby! Let me describe it to you...At the moment, the sun is setting over the glassy surfaced river, its orange light dazzlingly hits the mountains. These majestic mountain ranges seemed to reach all the way into the clouds. And, the captivating clouds above you are just sliding past the sky. The tricking lake is flowing through the picturesque meadow. Watching the baby ducklings follow their mother to the river is enchanting. The blooming meadow is flush with red, pink and purple flowers. Do you know, Annie darling? The view of the valley from the top of the mountain is breathtaking. I can see that a herd of sheep is slowly grazing over that bucolic valley. And..."

Annie closed Joseph's mouth with her long soft fingers. "Enough, I saw the ethereal appearance of nature through your beautiful words. It wouldn't have been that stunning even if I had seen it with my own eyes. You had described it in an awesome way. You never told me that you have this sort of talent."

Joseph gave a long sigh and stood up. He took a seat next to Annie, took hold of her hand and tightened it in his fists. Annie was able to feel the rigidness of the silver ring that Joseph had worn in his finger. She realized, it was the ring that she had gifted him on his birthday.

Annie hesitated and took off her hand from his, "Ehhh...I think it's getting late. Shall we leave now? I think mom must be waiting for us."

Joseph blushed and took hold of her hand again. "Why are you in a haste, Annie? Don't you like to spend some time with me?" he whispered into her ears.

"Ehhh... Nothing like that, Joe. You must have a lot of chores to do," Annie said hesitatingly.

"What is more important to me than being with you?"

Annie remained tight-lipped while Joseph cupped his palms on her cheeks. "Dear Annie, I am extremely sorry for hurting you like hell. Let's let go of everything like a nightmare. Can you please offer me a second chance in your life?" Joseph insisted so politely.

Annie was speechless. She never expected these words from Joseph. She thought that everything was gone. Her love, her eyesight, her job and ultimately, her life. She felt that all the blessings had returned back in a moment which she cannot accept at once.

"What happened to your ex-girlfriend?" Annie growled sarcastically.

Joseph tittered, "That's all gone. Will you promise me that you will never tell anyone about it?"

Annie promised and Joseph detailed the entire scene to her.

"Oh My God, Joseph. What has gone wrong with you? Won't you ever get the information of a girl before proposing to her?" Annie was surprised but she chuckled as well.

Joseph noticed Annie chuckling, "Am I a Joke to you?"

"I am sorry," Annie apologised.

"Anyway, let it go. Let's talk about our marriage. When shall we get married?" Joseph hurried.

"Excuse me, I never said 'yes' to your proposal," Annie retorted.

"What?"

"Yes, I have to think about it," Annie funnily swerved her face.

Joseph couldn't understand the sarcasm that Annie was playing with him. His face reddened with shrinks. "I think that I am the most unfortunate guy in this world. Anyway, let it go. It was my fault to reject you at the very beginning. Now, I badly need a second chance to fall in love with you for the first time but you aren't ready..."

Annie interrupted, "Joe, let me tell you one thing. Then and now, I always have the exact thing in my heart. I love you. I love only you. But remember one thing, I am a blind girl now."

"Annie, my love for Elena arouse from my eyes and it vanished very soon but my love for you had aroused from my heart and I assure you, it will never fade away," Joseph guaranteed Annie.

Annie blushed and nodded her head, "I trust you, Joe."

Joseph slowly approached closer to Annie and kissed her forehead. Subsequently, his lips got closer to hers but Annie pushed him a bit, "These love plays are allowed only after our marriage," Annie cautioned Joseph blushing cutely at him. Joseph silently took off his lips away from hers and asked, "Shall we go home?"

Annie nodded her head slightly.

"Not yours, mine. Amira must be waiting to welcome her favourite sister-in-law," Joseph said.

Annie nodded her head again and gave a bright smile.

www.ingramcontent.com/pod-product-compliance
Lightning Source LLC
Chambersburg PA
CBHW022059150726
47990CB00003B/1164